D0811171

MINI CLASSICS

THE
CAT THAT
WALKED BY
HIMSELF

RETOLD BY STEPHANIE LASLETT
ILLUSTRATED BY JO CAINE

PARRAGON

TITLES IN SERIES I AND II OF THE MINI CLASSICS INCLUDE:

SERIES I

Aladdin and the Magic Lamp
Ali Baba and the Forty Thieves
Alice in Wonderland
A Child's Garden of Verses
Cinderella
The Emperor's New Clothes
The Frog Prince
Goldilocks and the Three Bears
Hansel and Grettel
The Happy Prince
The Little Mermaid
Mother Goose's Rhymes
The Owl and the Pussycat (and other Nonsense Verse)
Puss in Boots
Sleeping Beauty
Snow White and the Seven Dwarfs
The Town Mouse and the Country Mouse (and other
    Aesop's Fables)
The Three Little Pigs
The Ugly Duckling
The Wizard of Oz

SERIES II

Beauty and the Beast
Brer Rabbit and Brer Fox
A Christmas Carol
The Hare and the Tortoise
How the Leopard Got His Spots
Jack and the Beanstalk
The Magic Carpet
The Night Before Christmas
Pinocchio
Rapunzel
Red Riding Hood
The Secret Garden
The Selfish Giant
Sinbad the Sailor
The Snow Queen
The Steadfast Tin Soldier
Thumbelina
The Walrus and the Carpenter
The Wind in the Willows I
The Wind in the Willows II

For Sarah — SL

A Parragon Book

Published by
Parragon Books,
Unit 13-17, Avonbridge Trading Estate,
Atlantic Road, Avonmouth, Bristol BS11 9QD

Produced by
The Templar Company plc,
Pippbrook Mill, London Road, Dorking, Surrey RH4 1JE

Copyright © 1995 Parragon Book Service Limited

All rights reserved

Designed by Mark Kingsley-Monks

Printed and bound in Great Britain

ISBN 1-85813-764-0

Hear and attend; for this befell and behappened, O Best Beloved, when the Tame animals were wild. The Dog was wild, and the Horse was wild, and the Cow was wild, and the Sheep was wild, and the Pig was wild — as wild as wild could be — and they walked in the Wet Wild Woods by their wild lones.

But the wildest of all the wild animals was the Cat. He walked by himself, and all places were alike to him.

Of course the Man was wild too. He was dreadfully wild. He didn't even begin to be tame till he met the Woman, and she told him that she did not like living in his wild ways. Instead of a heap of wet leaves, she found a nice dry Cave to lie down in; and she strewed clean sand on the floor; and she lit a nice fire of wood at the back of the Cave.

Then she hung a dried wild-horse skin, tail-down, across the opening of the cave; and she said, "Wipe your feet, dear, when you come in, and now we'll keep house."

That night, Best Beloved, they ate wild sheep roasted on the hot stones, and flavoured with wild garlic and wild pepper; and wild duck stuffed with wild rice; and wild cherries, and wild grenadillas. Then the Man went to sleep in front of the fire ever so happy; but the Woman sat up, combing her hair. She took the bone of the shoulder of mutton — the big flat blade-bone — and she looked at the wonderful marks on it, and she threw more wood on the fire, and she made magic. She made the First Singing Magic in the world.

Out in the Wet Wild Woods all the wild animals gathered together. They could see the bright light of the fire a long way off, and they wondered what it meant.

Wild Horse stamped with his wild foot and said, "O my Friends and O my Enemies, why have the Man and the Woman made that light in the cave, and what harm will it do us?"

Wild Dog lifted up his head and said, "I will go up and see and look. Cat, come with me."

"Nenni!" said the Cat. "I am the Cat who walks by

himself, and all places are alike to me. I will not come."

"Then we can never be friends again," said Wild Dog, and he trotted off to the cave. But then the cat said to himself. "All places are alike to me. Why should I not go too and see and look and come away at my own liking." So he slipped after Wild Dog softly, very softly and hid himself where he could hear everything.

When Wild Dog reached the mouth of the cave he lifted up the dried horse-skin with his nose and sniffed the beautiful smell of the roast mutton, and the woman heard him, and laughed, and said, "Here comes the first. Wild Thing out of the Wild Woods, what do you want?"

Wild Dog said, "O my Enemy and Wife of my Enemy, what is this that smells so good in the Wild Woods?"

Then the Woman picked up a roasted mutton bone and threw it to Wild Dog, and said, "Wild Thing out of the Wild Woods, taste and try." Wild Dog gnawed the bone, and it was so delicious he said "O my

Enemy and Wife of my Enemy, give me another."

The Woman said, "Wild Thing out of the Wild Woods, help my Man to hunt through the day and guard this Cave at night, and I will give you as many roast bones as you need."

"Ah!" said the Cat, listening. "This is a very wise Woman, but she is not so wise as I am."

Wild Dog crawled into the Cave and laid his head on the Woman's lap, and said, "O my Friend and Wife of my Friend, I will help your Man to hunt through the day, and at night I will guard your cave."

"Ah!" said the Cat. "That is a very foolish Dog." And he went back through the Wet Wild Woods, but he never told anybody.

23

When the Man woke up
he said. "What is Wild Dog
doing here?" And the

Woman said, "His name is not Wild Dog any more, but the First Friend, because he will be our friend for always and always and always. Take him with you when you go hunting."

Next night the Woman
cut great green armfuls of
fresh grass from the water-
meadows, and dried it
before the fire so that it
smelt like new-mown hay,
and she sat at the mouth of
the Cave and plaited a
halter out of horse-hide,
and she looked at the
mutton bone — at the big
broad blade-bone — and
she made a Magic.

She made the Second Singing Magic in the world. Out in the Wild Woods all the wild animals wondered what had happened to the Wild Dog, and at last Wild Horse stamped with his foot and said, "I will go and see and say why Wild Dog has not returned. Cat, come with me."

"Nenni!" said the Cat. "I am the Cat who walks by

himself, and all places are alike to me. I will not come." But all the same he followed Wild Horse softly, very softly, and hid himself where he could hear everything.

When the Woman heard Wild Horse tripping and stumbling on his long mane, she laughed and said, "Here comes the second. Wild Thing out of the Wild Woods, what do you want?"

Wild Horse said, "O my Enemy and Wife of my Enemy, where is Wild Dog?"

The Woman laughed and said, "Wild Thing out of the Wild Woods, you did not come here for Wild Dog, but for the sake of this good grass."

And Wild Horse, tripping and stumbling on his long

mane, said, "That is true; give it me to eat."

The Woman said, "Wild Thing out of the Wild Woods, bend your wild head and wear what I give you, and you shall eat the wonderful grass three times a day."

"Ah!" said the Cat, listening. "This is a clever Woman, but she is not so clever as I am."

Wild Horse bent his wild head, and the Woman slipped the plaited halter over it, and Wild Horse breathed on the woman's feet and said, "O my Mistress, and Wife of my Master, I will be your servant for the sake of the wonderful grass."

"Ah!" said the Cat. "That is a very foolish Horse." And he went back through the Wet Wild Woods, but he never told anybody.

When the Man and the
Dog came back from
hunting, the Man said,
"What is Wild Horse doing
here?"

And the Woman said, "His
name is not Wild Horse any
more, but the First Servant,
because he will carry us
from place to place for
always and always and
always. Ride on his back
when you go hunting."

Next day, holding her wild head high so that her wild horns should not catch in the wild trees, Wild Cow came up to the cave.

The Cat followed and hid just the same as before and everything happened just the same as before; and when Wild Cow had promised to give her milk to the Woman every day in exchange for the wonderful grass, the Cat went back through the Wet Wild Woods, but he never told anybody.

And when the Man and

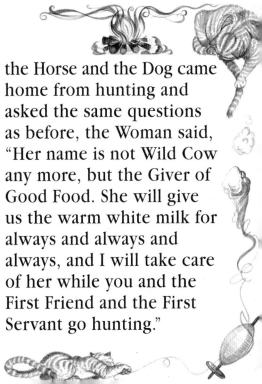

the Horse and the Dog came home from hunting and asked the same questions as before, the Woman said, "Her name is not Wild Cow any more, but the Giver of Good Food. She will give us the warm white milk for always and always and always, and I will take care of her while you and the First Friend and the First Servant go hunting."

Next day the Cat waited
to see if any other Wild
Thing would go up to the
Cave, but no one moved in
the Wet Wild Woods; all
was quiet and still.

So the Cat walked there
by himself; and he saw the
Woman milking the Cow,
and he saw the light of the
fire in the Cave, and he
smelt the smell of the
warm milk.

Cat said, "O my Enemy and Wife of my Enemy, where did Wild Cow go?"

The Woman laughed and said, "Wild Thing out of the Wild Woods, go back to the Woods again, for I have braided up my hair, and I have put away the magic blade-bone, and we have no more need of either friends or servants in our Cave."

Cat said, "I am not a friend and I am not a servant. No, I am the Cat who walks by himself, and I wish to come into your cave."

The Woman said, "Then why did you not come with First Friend on the first night?" The Cat was angry but the Woman laughed. "You are the Cat who walks by himself, and all places are alike to you. You are neither friend nor servant. You have said it yourself. Go away and walk by yourself in all places alike."

Then Cat pretended to be sorry and said, "Must I never come into the Cave? Must I never sit by the warm fire? Must I never drink the warm white milk? You are very wise and beautiful. You should not be cruel, even to a Cat."

The Woman said, "I knew
I was wise, but I did not
know I was beautiful. So I
will make a bargain with
you. If ever I say one word
in your praise, you may
come into the Cave."

"And if you say two words
in my praise?" said the Cat.

"I never shall," said the
Woman, "but if I say two
words in your praise, you
may sit by the fire."

"And if you say three words?" said the Cat.

"I never shall," said the Woman, "but if I say three words in your praise, you may drink the warm white milk three times a day for always and always and always."

Then the Cat arched his
back and went away through
the Wet Wild Woods waving
his wild tail and walking by
his wild lone.

That night when the Man
and the Horse and the Dog
came home from hunting,
the Woman did not tell
them of the bargain that
she had made with the Cat,
because she was afraid that
they might not like it.

Cat went far away and hid himself in the Wet Wild Woods by his wild lone for a long time till the Woman forgot all about him. Only the Bat — the little upside-down Bat — that hung inside the Cave knew where the Cat hid; and every evening Bat would fly to Cat with news of what was happening.

One evening Bat said,

"There is a Baby in the Cave. He is new and pink and fat and small, and the Woman is very fond of him."

"Ah!" said the Cat. "But what is the baby fond of?"

"He is fond of things that are soft and tickle," said the Bat. "He is fond of warm things to hold in his arms when he goes to sleep. He is fond of being played with. He likes all those things."

"Ah!" said the Cat. "Then my time has come."

Next night Cat hid very near the Cave till morning-time, and Man and Dog and Horse went hunting. The Woman was busy cooking that morning, and the baby cried and interrupted. So she carried him outside the Cave and gave him some pebbles to play with. But still the Baby cried.

Then the Cat put out his
paddy paw and patted
the Baby on the cheek,
and it cooed; and the
Cat rubbed against its fat
knees and tickled it
under its fat chin with his
tail. And the Baby laughed;
and the Woman heard him
and smiled.

Then the Bat — the little upside-down Bat — that hung in the mouth of the Cave said, "O my Hostess and Wife of my Host and Mother of my Host's Son, a Wild Thing from the Wild Woods is most beautifully playing with your Baby."

"A blessing on that Wild Thing whoever he may be," said the Woman, "for I was a busy woman this morning and he has done me a service."

That very minute and second, Best Beloved, the dried horse-skin Curtain that was stretched tail-down at the mouth of the Cave fell down — *woosh!*-because it remembered the bargain the woman had made with the Cat; and when she went to pick it up — lo and behold! — the

Cat was sitting quite comfy
inside the Cave.

"O my Enemy and Wife of
my Enemy and Mother of
my Enemy," said the Cat, "it
is I: for you have spoken a
word of praise, and now I
sit within the Cave for
always and always and
always. But still I am the
Cat who walks by himself,
and all places are alike to
me."

The Woman was very angry, and shut her lips tight and took up her spinning-wheel and began to spin.

But the small Baby cried because the Cat had gone away, and the woman could not hush it, for it struggled and kicked and grew black in the face.

"O my Enemy and Wife of my Enemy and Mother of

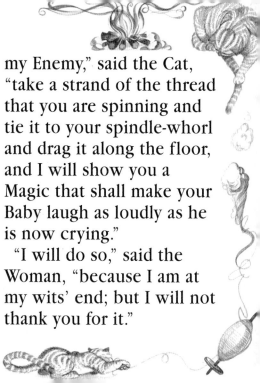

my Enemy," said the Cat, "take a strand of the thread that you are spinning and tie it to your spindle-whorl and drag it along the floor, and I will show you a Magic that shall make your Baby laugh as loudly as he is now crying."

"I will do so," said the Woman, "because I am at my wits' end; but I will not thank you for it."

She tied the thread to the little clay spindle-whorl and drew it across the floor, and the Cat ran after it and patted it with his paws and rolled head over heels, and tossed it this way and that way over his shoulder and chased it between his hind legs and pretended to lose it, and pounced down upon it again, till the Baby laughed as loudly as it had been crying, and scrambled after the Cat and frolicked all over the Cave till it grew tired and settled down to sleep with the Cat in its arms.

"Now," said the Cat, "I will sing the Baby a song that shall keep him asleep for an hour." And he began to purr, loud and low, low and loud, till the Baby fell

ast asleep. The Woman
miled as she looked down
pon the two of them, and
aid, "That was wonderfully
one. No question but you
re very clever, O Cat."
That very minute and
econd, Best Beloved, the
moke of the fire at the
ack of the Cave came
own in clouds from the
oof — *puff!* — because it
emembered the bargain

she had made with the Cat;
and when it had cleared
away — lo and behold! —
the Cat was sitting quite
comfy close to the fire.

"O my Enemy and Wife of
my Enemy, and Mother of
my Enemy," said the Cat, "it
is I: for you have spoken a
second word in my praise,
and now I can sit by the
warm fire at the back of
the Cave for always and

always and always. But still I am the Cat who walks by himself, and all places are alike to me."

72

Then the Woman was
very very angry and let
down her hair and put
more wood on the fire and
brought out the broad
blade-bone of the shoulder
of mutton and began to
make a Magic that should
prevent her from saying a
third word in praise of the
Cat. By and by the Cave
grew so still that a little
wee-wee mouse crept out

of a corner and ran across the floor. "O my Enemy and Wife of my Enemy and Mother of my Enemy," said the Cat, "is that little mouse part of your Magic?"

"Ouh! Chee! No indeed!" said the Woman, and she jumped upon the foot-stool in front of the fire and braided up her hair very quick for fear that the mouse should run up it.

"Ah," said the Cat. "Then the mouse will do me no harm?" "No, eat it quickly," said the Woman, "and I will ever be grateful to you."

Cat made one jump and caught the little mouse, and the Woman said, "A hundred thanks. Even the First Friend is not quick enough to catch little mice as you have done. You must be very wise."

That very minute and second, O Best Beloved, the Milk-pot crackled in two pieces — *ffft!* — because it remembered the bargain she had made with the Cat; and when the Woman jumped down from the footstool — lo and behold! — the Cat was lapping up the warm white milk that lay in one of the broken pieces.

"O my Enemy and Wife of my Enemy and Mother of my Enemy, " said the Cat, "it is I: for you have spoken three words in my praise, and now I can drink the warm white milk three times a day for always and always and always. But *still* I am the Cat who walks by himself, and all places are alike to me.

Then the Woman laughed and set the Cat a bowl of the warm white milk and said, "O Cat, you are as clever as a man, but remember that your bargain was not made with the Man or the Dog, and I do not know what they will do when they come home."

"What is that to me?" said the Cat. "If I have my place in the Cave by the fire and my warm white milk three times a day I do not care what the Man or the Dog can do."

That evening when the Man and the Dog came into the Cave, the Woman told them all the story of the bargain, while the Cat sat by the fire and smiled. Then the Man said, "Yes, but he has not made a bargain with *me*."

Then he took off his two leather boots and he took up his little stone axe (that makes three) and he fetched a piece of wood and a hatchet (that is five altogether), and he set them out in a row and he said, "Now we will make *our* bargain. If you do not catch mice when you are in the Cave for always and always and always, I will

throw these five things at
you whenever I see you,
and so shall all proper Men
do after me."

"Ah!" said the Woman,
listening. "This is a very
clever Cat, but he is not so
clever as my Man."

The Cat counted the five
things and said "*Still* I am
the Cat who walks by
himself, and all places are
alike to me."

"Not when I am near," said the Man. "If you had not said that last I would have put all these things away for always and always and always; but now I am going to throw my two boots and my little stone axe at you whenever I meet you. And so shall all proper Men do after me!"

Then the Dog said, "Wait a minute. He has not made

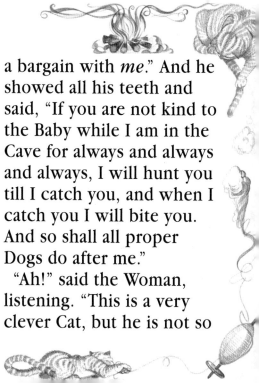

a bargain with *me*." And he showed all his teeth and said, "If you are not kind to the Baby while I am in the Cave for always and always and always, I will hunt you till I catch you, and when I catch you I will bite you. And so shall all proper Dogs do after me."

"Ah!" said the Woman, listening. "This is a very clever Cat, but he is not so clever as the Dog."

Cat counted the Dog's teeth and he said, "*Still* I am the Cat who walks by himself, and all places are alike to me."

"Not when I am near," said the Dog. "You should not have said that last bit. Now I am going to hunt you up a tree whenever I meet you. And so shall all proper Dogs do after me."

Then the Man threw his two boots and the little stone axe (that makes three) at the Cat, and the Cat ran out of the Cave and the Dog chased him up a tree; and from that day to this, Best Beloved, three proper Men out of five will always throw things at a Cat whenever they meet him, and all proper Dogs will chase him up a tree.

But the Cat keeps his side of the bargain too. He will kill mice, and he will be kind to Babies when he is in the house, just as long as they do not pull his tail too hard.

But when he has done that, and between times, and when the moon gets up and night comes, he is the Cat that walks by himself, and all places are alike to him.

Then he goes out to the Wet Wild Woods or up the Wet Wild Trees or on the Wet Wild Roofs, waving his wild tail and walking by his wild lone.

RUDYARD KIPLING

The *Just So* stories by Rudyard Kipling
(1865-1936) have delighted children for
generations with their far-fetched
explanations of how animals came
to acquire their peculiar characteristics.
Kipling may well have got the idea from
the Uncle Remus stories of Joel Chandler
Harris, such as "Why Mr Possum has no
Hair upon his Tail".